DC SUPER HERO FAIRY TALES

BLACK CANARY
AND THE THREE BAD BEARS

by Laurie S. Sutton
illustrated by Agnes Garbowska
colors by Sil Brys

Published by Stone Arch Books, an imprint of Capstone
1710 Roe Crest Drive, North Mankato, Minnesota 56003
capstonepub.com

Library of Congress Cataloging-in-Publication Data
Names: Sutton, Laurie, author. | Garbowska, Agnes, illustrator. |
Brys, Silvana, colorist.
Title: Black Canary and the three bad bears / by Laurie S. Sutton ;
illustrated by Agnes Garbowska ; colors by Sil Brys.
Description: North Mankato, Minnesota : Stone Arch Books, an imprint of
Capstone, [2022] | Series: DC super hero fairy tales | Audience: Ages 8–11. |
Audience: Grades 4–6. | Summary: In this twisted retelling of "Goldilocks
and the Three Bears," Superhero Black Canary sneaks into the hideout of
three villains and battles booby traps and evil machines to save the world.
Identifiers: LCCN 2021029686 (print) | LCCN 2021029687 (ebook) |
ISBN 9781663959058 (hardcover) | ISBN 9781666329018 (paperback) |
ISBN 9781666329025 (pdf)
Subjects: LCSH: Black Canary (Fictitious character)—Juvenile fiction. |
Superheroes—Juvenile fiction. | Supervillains—Juvenile fiction. |
Theft—Juvenile fiction. | Control (Psychology)—Juvenile fiction. | CYAC:
Superheroes—Fiction. | Supervillains—Fiction. | LCGFT: Superhero fiction.
Classification: LCC PZ7.S968294 Bj 2022 (print) | LCC PZ7.S968294 (ebook) |
DDC 813.54 [Fic]—dc23
LC record available at https://lccn.loc.gov/2021029686
LC ebook record available at https://lccn.loc.gov/2021029687

Designed by Hilary Wacholz

Printed and bound in the USA. PO4608

TABLE OF CONTENTS

UNCE UPON A TIME ...

THE WORLD'S GREATEST
SUPER HEROES COLLIDED WITH
THE WORLD'S BEST-KNOWN
FAIRY TALES TO CREATE ...

DC SUPER HERO
FAIRY TALES

Now, Black Canary is sneaking into the hideout of three villains. She'll have to get everything just right to defeat the trio and their evil scheme in this twisted retelling of "Goldilocks and the Three Bears"!

CHAPTER 1

THREE AGAINST ONE

Black Canary rode her motorcycle along the nighttime streets of the city. She was on patrol. She was a Super Hero with amazing vocal powers and martial arts abilities, and it was her job to go out looking for trouble. She always seemed to find it.

SHREEE! SHREEE! SHREEE!

That's a burglar alarm! And it's coming from nearby, Canary thought as she sped in the direction of the shrill sound.

It was only two short blocks before Canary reached the alleyway behind the MegaTech factory building. She quickly saw the reason for the alarm. The heavy metal garage doors on a loading dock had been torn apart as if they were made of cardboard.

Now that's what I call a forced entry, Black Canary thought. *But who—or what—has the strength to do that?*

The hero got off her motorcycle and flattened her back against the side of the building. She slowly made her way over to get a closer look. She took deep breaths, ready to fill her lungs and unleash her sonic Canary Cry.

Suddenly a fifteen-foot-tall woman came out of the opening, ducking under the top of the ten-foot-tall doors. She had long, red hair and wore a pink tunic.

The giant woman carried a stack of wooden packing crates. They looked like toy blocks in her large arms. After stepping off the loading dock, she turned and used a fist to smash the screeching alarm.

"Shut up!" the woman said.

That's the Super-Villain Giganta! Black Canary realized. *I recognize her from the Justice League files. She can grow to enormous size and has incredible strength. At least now I know who was strong enough to wreck that door.*

The hero wasn't about to let the crook get away with whatever was in the crates. She stepped forward and let loose her Canary Cry.

EEEEEEEEEEEEEEEEEEEEE!

The wave of sound hit Giganta like a tsunami. The villain was knocked off her feet. The crates went skidding out of her reach.

"I don't know what you're up to, Giganta, but I'm putting a stop to it," Black Canary said.

She was about to deliver a knockout Canary Cry when a new sight caught her off guard. A second Super-Villain stepped out of the building and onto the loading dock! He looked like a gorilla but was as big as a bear. He was carrying a stack of wooden crates in his arms as easily as Giganta had.

"Gorilla Grodd!" Black Canary shouted, startled.

She did not need the Justice League files to know about this foe. Grodd had the body of a great ape and the mind of a genius. But instead of using his super-intelligence for good, he used it to plot evil schemes against humanity.

"Well, well, well. I see a certain little songbird has been messing with my mission," said Gorilla Grodd.

Black Canary did not hesitate this time. She sent a powerful Canary Cry straight at the simian Super-Villain.

EEEEEEEEEEEEEEEEE!

Grodd held up his crates as a shield against the sonic blast.

CRAAACK!

The wooden boxes shattered, but they protected Grodd. The ape looked down at the broken bits of high-tech equipment that had been inside. He did not look happy.

"*Grrrr!* I needed those parts," Grodd growled.

The primate picked up a large chunk of wrecked machinery and threw it at Black Canary. She leaped out of the way using her acrobatic skills. But that brought her within reach of Giganta! The supersized Super-Villain tried to pound the hero with a giant fist.

WHOOOMP!

Black Canary dodged the blow.

"We don't have time for games!" Gorilla Grodd called. "Giganta, get back to the lab. Grundy can take care of this annoying bird."

Grundy? Black Canary thought, surprised. *There are three of them?*

She quickly spun around to see a third Super-Villain. Solomon Grundy was getting ready to jump off the loading dock.

The large, immortal zombie had an undead mind that was simple and childlike. But his superhuman strength made him a terrible threat.

Black Canary drew in a breath too late. Grundy slammed into her before she could let loose a sonic scream.

THWUUUMP!

She fell to the ground, stunned.

"It looks like the canary has stopped singing," Gorilla Grodd said. "Finish her, Grundy."

As Grodd and Giganta walked away from the crime scene, Solomon Grundy picked up the dazed hero.

"Little bird is broken," Grundy mumbled. "Put you in trash."

The simpleminded Super-Villain opened the lid of a dumpster and tossed the hero inside. Then he dropped the lid and lumbered away.

Black Canary lay in the dark for a few moments to catch her breath. When she finally did, she did not like the smells that surrounded her. The hero climbed out of the dumpster as fast as she could. She was just in time to see Solomon Grundy slowly turning the corner at the end of the alley.

Grodd told Giganta to get back to the lab, Canary thought. *That must be where Grundy is going. I can follow him there and find out what these three bearish brutes are up to. It can't be good if more than one villain is involved.*

Black Canary secretly trailed behind Solomon Grundy.

Soon, Grundy had led the hero to a large warehouse. It was a simple brick building that blended in with all the other structures around it. Canary watched as Grundy opened a plain metal door and went inside.

A few moments later, the whole trio of troublemakers stepped back outside. The metal door slammed shut as Gorilla Grodd gave new orders to his crew.

"Let's go to the Cyber-Systems factory across town. It should have the equipment I need," Grodd said. "Black Canary delayed my plan, but she didn't stop it. The city will be under our control before dawn."

Before dawn? That doesn't leave me much time to put an end to Grodd's scheme—whatever it is, Canary thought. *But first I have to get inside their hideout. If I can't handle the situation myself, I'll call in the Justice League.*

Black Canary watched the villains leave and then crept over to the metal door of the warehouse. She turned the knob. It was unlocked.

Okay, that's suspicious, Canary thought.

Prepared for anything, she stepped inside and shut the door behind her. She saw that she was in a hallway. A single light bulb hung on the ceiling. A pair of elevator doors stood at the end of the hall. Canary walked slowly toward the elevator doors.

CLAAAANG! CLAAAANG!

Suddenly two thick metal barriers dropped down from the ceiling on either side of her.

It's a trap! Black Canary realized just as the "light bulb" spewed out a cloud of bright green gas.

CHAPTER 2

TRIPLE TROUBLE

Black Canary quickly held her breath as the green gas started to fill the small space.

I have enough breath for only one Canary Cry, she thought. *I need to make it count.*

She pounded her fists on the metal barrier, the wall, and the floor. She listened to the differences in the sounds.

THUMP! WHUMP! THUMP!

The wall is the thinnest, Canary decided. *It will be the easiest to break through.*

EEEEEEEEEEEEEEEEEE!

The hero's single sonic blast cracked the
wood and plaster of the wall. Black Canary
used her shoulder to break through the rest
of the way. She stumbled into what looked
like a big, empty storage room. It was large
enough to let the green gas thin out and
become harmless.

Black Canary took deep breaths as she
glanced around the room. *There's nothing
in here that gives me a clue to what those three
baddies are planning,* she thought. *And where
is all the high-tech equipment they're stealing?
I have to keep searching.*

Canary headed over to a door on the far
side of the room. The door opened on rusty
hinges to reveal the top of a staircase. It led
down into darkness.

I hope I'm not walking into another trap. But I don't have time to be cautious, the hero thought. She put her foot on the first step. *Here goes nothing.*

The old wood groaned, but nothing else happened. Black Canary hurried down the stairs and came into another hallway. A single light bulb hung on the ceiling. A pair of elevator doors stood at the far end.

This looks familiar, Canary thought.

EEEEEEEEEEE!

Black Canary aimed a sonic scream at the light bulb. The bulb burst, but no gas came out. The hallway plunged into darkness.

Well, the good thing is, this wasn't another gas trap, Canary thought. *The bad thing is, now I can't see anything.*

Putting one hand on the wall to guide herself, Canary started to inch forward. She had gone only a few feet when a strange noise echoed in the hall.

WHIIIR! WHIIIR!

That doesn't sound good, Canary thought, struggling to see through the darkness.

Suddenly a cold metal something grabbed one of her wrists. A second later, another something wrapped around her waist. Black Canary was quickly pinned against the wall. She looked down at her waist and saw the faint shape of a metal tentacle.

WHIIIR! WHIIIR!

She could hear more metal clanking coming toward her in the dark.

EEEEEEEEEEEEEE!

The Super Hero let out a wide wave of sound in all directions. She did not know exactly what she was fighting, but she fought all the same.

She repeated her Canary Cry. She twisted back and forth, trying to break free of the things that held her to the wall.

VRRRMMMMM! SPAAARK! BOOOOM!

Black Canary's sonic song finally vibrated the metal foes to their breaking point. Their inner wirings sparked and exploded. Canary heard heavy objects fall onto the floor. The metal tentacles holding her went limp.

DING!

The elevator doors opened automatically. Light from inside the elevator spilled into the dark hallway.

At last, Black Canary could see what she had been fighting. Or, at least what was left of what she had been fighting.

Shattered metal pieces were scattered all over the hall. The two tentacles that had held Canary now hung against the wall. They looked like thick metal earthworms.

These traps are no joke! Gorilla Grodd is taking serious steps to protect whatever he and his gang are doing here, Black Canary realized. *That makes it all the more important for me to find out what that is and to stop it.*

The Super Hero stepped into the elevator and looked at the buttons on the control panel. The bottom one was marked *LAB*.

The only way to go from here is down, Canary thought. She pressed the bottom button.

The elevator lowered quietly. Then the doors opened up into yet another hallway. But it was different than the others Canary had faced.

This hall was very, very long. The walls, floor, and ceiling were made of square metal plates. Small spotlights were tucked up into the ceiling randomly and created little pools of light on the floor. At the end of the hall was a single door with the word *LAB* in bright red letters.

"Okay, now this is *definitely* suspicious," Canary muttered.

She looked down at the circle of light on the floor just outside the elevator doors. She wondered if it would trigger whatever trap the hallway was hiding. There was only one way to find out.

Expecting the worst, Black Canary bravely stepped out of the elevator and into the light.

Nothing happened. She took another step forward, out of the light.

The metal panels on the floor, ceiling, and walls opened all at once to reveal the tops of giant pistons. They shot out and started slamming into each other.

BWAAANG! BWAAANG! BWAAANG!

Black Canary froze. Then she stepped backward into the light.

THWUUUNK! THWUUUNK! THWUUUNK!

The pistons pulled back, and the panels closed.

The light didn't trigger the trap. It stopped it! Canary realized as she stood in the pool of light by the elevator.

She looked out at the other bright spots scattered down the rest of the hallway.

The lights are safety zones, Canary thought. *So, all I have to do is get past the pistons and reach the lights, one by one, to work my way through the course.*

Black Canary took a deep breath. Then she sprinted out toward the nearest spot of light.

BWAAANG! BWAAANG! BWAAANG!

All the metal panels flew open. The giant pistons came out and crashed against each other.

Black Canary was almost smashed by the first pair. But using her amazing acrobatic skills, she rolled out of the way.

EEEEEEEEEEEEEEEE!

She used her sonic scream to crack the next piston. Then she delivered a flying kick to shatter the weakened metal. Canary slid along the floor and reached the next safety zone of light.

The pistons stopped. They slid back into the walls, ceiling, and floor.

One down, Black Canary thought. She counted the string of spotlights ahead of her. *And twenty to go. Grodd and his gang are not making this easy for me. And I'm running out of time!*

CHAPTER 3

THE GANG'S ALL HERE

I thought the first two traps were hard, but this one is the hardest, Black Canary thought. *I have to get through it quickly, before the three villains return home!*

Black Canary carefully inched outside the circle of light. The metal pistons flew out and resumed their pounding.

BWAAANG! BWAAANG! BWAAANG!

The Super Hero let out a tremendous Canary Cry toward the clanging metal.

EEEEEEEEEEEEEEEEE!

The nearest pistons shattered under the sonic attack, but the others did not. The path ahead was still dangerous. Black Canary studied the metal pistons as they slammed and smashed into each other.

There's a pattern! Canary realized. *The pistons come out of the wall, ceiling, wall, then floor. If I time my run just right, I can avoid them.*

Black Canary darted forward. She ducked under a piston surging out of the opposite wall and slid along the floor. A piston shot down from the ceiling. It pounded the floor close to her ear. Canary grabbed the rod, swung around it, and leaped to her feet.

Wall, ceiling, wall, floor, she reminded herself as the next piston came out of the wall.

Canary jumped over it. She landed smoothly and sped past the next piston before it pushed out of the floor.

The hero worked her way down the hallway, using her acrobatic skills and Canary Cry to dodge or destroy the mechanical menaces. *Wall, ceiling, wall, floor. Wall, ceiling, wall, floor,* she repeated in her mind to keep track of the pattern.

At last, Black Canary reached the final safety zone. She paused, a little out of breath. She looked back down the hallway at the trail of wreckage she had left behind.

Well, that was a challenge! But I beat everything the three villains put in my way, Canary thought. *It's time I finally find out what schemes they're planning on the other side of this door.*

Black Canary opened the unlocked door and walked into the lab. The large room hummed with electronics. In the center stood three large computer banks. Cables and wires connected the computers to each other. Monitors displayed complex graphs. A shiny metal helmet sat on a nearby shelf. Canary recognized the helmet immediately.

That's Grodd's mind-control helmet! she thought. *He uses it to make humans obey his commands. It must be part of his plan.*

As Black Canary walked toward the computers, she noticed large sections of the machines were unfinished. Many of the panels were open, and twisted wires were sticking out. Other portions were completely empty on the inside. Tools lay scattered on the floor.

Whatever these machines are for, Grodd and his gang aren't done building them, Canary realized. *That's why they were robbing the MegaTech factory. They needed more parts. Well, a few extra pieces won't help after I'm finished.*

EEEEEEEEEEEEEEE!

Black Canary let out a sonic Canary Cry toward one of the computer banks. *BLAAAAM!* It exploded.

That was easy, Black Canary thought.

She aimed another Canary Cry at the second bank of computers. *SPUUT! SPUUT!* The monitors sparked and fizzled, but most of the electronics were undamaged.

That was harder, Black Canary realized.

A third Canary Cry had no effect on the last bank of computers.

Hmm. That one was hardest of all, Black Canary thought.

She knew that the machines had to be destroyed or shut down—fast. The three villains could return at any moment.

Black Canary grabbed one of the three thick cables connecting the last two computer banks. She started pulling.

Since my Canary Cry didn't work on these, maybe some good, old-fashioned muscle will, she thought.

It took several tugs, but the cable finally came free. *SKZAAT!* The cable sparked as the connection broke. The electrical charge stung Canary. She dropped the cable and rubbed her hands.

"Ow," she muttered.

Canary grasped the second cable. It was harder to disconnect. She had to brace one foot against the side of the machine before the cable pulled away. *SKZAAT! SKZAAT!*

"Ow, ow!" she yelped.

The hero reached for the final cable. She pulled with all her strength. But again, the third was the hardest of all. She let out a short Canary Cry at the stubborn connector.

EEEEEE!

The cable finally came apart from the machine, but a mighty surge of energy came with it! The electricity raced down the cable and struck Black Canary. *SKZAAAAAT!* She was instantly knocked out and fell to the floor.

Gorilla Grodd, Giganta, and Solomon Grundy returned to the warehouse hideout. Each crook carried crates of stolen electronic equipment. As soon as they opened the outside door, the trio saw the metal barrier blocking the hallway.

"Looks like somebody snuck into our lair and triggered the gas trap," Grodd said. "Let's see who it is."

The primate put his palm on a section of the wall next to the door. A hidden panel popped open, and Grodd pressed a button inside. Both metal barriers in the hall rose back into the ceiling.

"Well, it looks like 'somebody' smashed a hole in the wall to escape," Giganta said.

"Ha! They get scared and run away," Grundy said.

But when the three got to the floor below, they saw that the second trap had also been sprung. Pieces of the metal tentacles littered the floor.

"Whoa! Who could have done this?" Giganta asked.

"Somebody very strong," Grundy said.

"It seems that the intruder didn't run away after all," Grodd said. "There's one more trap. I'm sure it caught our uninvited guest."

Grodd led the group to the last trap. They quickly discovered that most of it had also been destroyed. The few undamaged pistons were frozen in midmotion.

"Look. Somebody got in lab," Grundy said, pointing to the open door at the end of the hall.

With a growl, Gorilla Grodd dropped his crates of stolen equipment and charged down the hallway. Giganta and Grundy followed him past the unmoving pistons. All three ran into the lab, ready for battle. They were surprised to find a blonde woman lying on the floor.

"Somebody got in, and there she is," Giganta said.

"Black Canary!" Grodd grunted. "*Hmph.* It seems we have an unexpected Goldilocks in our lair."

Grundy poked Black Canary with a large finger. "Little bird is asleep."

"Tie her up," Grodd ordered. "She worked so hard to thwart my plan. Now she will be a part of it."

CHAPTER 4

FAMILY FEUD

Black Canary woke up to see Solomon Grundy's gray face inches from hers. His pale eyes stared at her unblinkingly.

The hero immediately tried to deliver a Canary Cry against the villain. But no sound came out. A metal band was strapped over her mouth like a mask. She tried to take it off, but she found more metal bands were holding her arms to a chair. She had been caught!

"Little bird is awake!" Grundy called, taking a step back.

At the damaged computer banks, Gorilla Grodd set down his tools. He stomped over to his captive.

"Well, well. Look who has been sleeping in my secret lab," Grodd said.

"You won't get away with this," Black Canary managed to mumble through the band across her mouth.

"Oh, but I can," Grodd replied. "You may have broken some equipment, but it can be repaired. My plan will still succeed on time."

"Plan? What plan?" Black Canary asked.

"Grodd! Don't tell her the plan!" Giganta warned from where she was adding new electronic parts to the second computer bank.

"I have everything under control," Grodd replied, annoyed. "She can't stop us now."

Giganta rolled her eyes as she turned back to her repairs. "If I had a dollar for every time I heard a Super-Villain say that, I would be rich and retired," she muttered.

Black Canary let out a sigh and said, "You're right, Grodd. Tied up like this, I can't do anything to stop you." She let her body sag in the chair.

Canary pretended to be defeated. But every time she spoke, she secretly tested the limits of the metal band. She was realizing that it blocked the high frequency sound of her Canary Cry. However, low frequency sounds, like normal speech, went through.

She could use that to her advantage. First, she needed to cause a distraction.

"So, what now?" the hero asked.

"When the repairs are complete, I'll connect these machines to my mind-control helmet," Grodd said, pointing to the shiny metal helmet resting on the shelf. Then he tapped his finger on top of Canary's head. "I'll broadcast a massive mind-control wave to every human within a thousand miles. Everyone will obey Gorilla Grodd. Starting with you."

Black Canary raised an eyebrow. "That's all? No taking over the world?"

"This is just phase one," Grodd replied. "First, I will become king of a new Grodd Nation. Giganta will be my queen. Grundy wants to be a prince."

"Grundy gets crown," the undead villain added with a grin.

"Then, I will use my human subjects to build an even bigger machine and use it to control the continent," Grodd boasted. "After that, the whole world will be mine!"

"Yours? What about Giganta and Grundy?" Canary asked.

"Grundy want Australia!" Solomon Grundy said.

"Don't worry, Grundy. You can have Australia," Grodd replied.

"Grundy like kangaroos," the big brute added with a chuckle.

"Australia is basically all desert," Canary said. "What does Giganta get, the Sahara?"

That caught Giganta's attention. She stopped her work on the mind-control machinery and turned to face Gorilla Grodd.

"You know, we never discussed who gets what," Giganta said. She frowned and put her hands on her hips. "I'm not doing any more work on this stuff until I know exactly what's in it for me."

"*Grrr*. I promise that you can have whatever you want," Grodd growled.

"Promises? From a Super-Villain? Ha!" Giganta laughed.

"Just get back to work," Grodd ordered. "I need my machines complete before I can launch phase one."

"*You* need *your* machines complete before *you* can launch phase one? See what I mean? It's all about *you*!" Giganta replied angrily. She folded her arms across her chest. "*We* are going to settle this right now. Grundy! Get over here!"

Black Canary watched the three villains gather on the other side of the lab. Their arguing was loud, just as she had hoped.

My strategy worked. My comment about Giganta getting the Sahara as her "reward" made her doubt Gorilla Grodd, Canary thought. *Now they're not paying any attention to me.*

While the trio was distracted, Black Canary tested the strength of the metal band over her mouth. She started to hum.

HMMMM! HMMMMMM!

She used her vocal powers to begin with a low frequency sound. Then she slowly increased the frequency until it was just right. She felt the band vibrating. She could feel it breaking.

Almost there! Black Canary thought as she continued to hum.

A moment later, the metal band snapped. It fell away from Canary's face. It took only another moment to focus a shot of sound on the metal straps that held her to the chair. It wasn't a full-strength Canary Cry, but it did the job. The straps dropped onto the floor.

CLAAANG! CLAAAANG!

"Wait! What was that?" Giganta asked, turning toward the sound of the falling metal.

All three villains stopped their bickering as soon as they saw that their foe was free. They rushed forward.

Black Canary stood at the ready. She braced herself to battle Grodd, Giganta, and Grundy.

EEEEEEEEEEEE!

The hero slammed the trio back with a powerful Canary Cry. The sonic blast threw them off their feet and against the computer banks.

Gorilla Grodd recovered first and leaped toward the hero. He reached out to grab Black Canary, but she twisted out of the way. Grodd could not stop his attack midair.

CRRUUUNCH!

The ape crashed into the far wall and slumped to the floor, leaving behind a large dent in the plaster.

Giganta increased her size until she almost touched the ceiling. The floor shook as she stomped across the room. Solomon Grundy raced alongside her. They charged toward Black Canary like a pair of military tanks.

Black Canary ran straight at them.
At the last second, she dropped into a slide
and skidded between Giganta's legs. As she
did, Canary kicked the giant foe's feet out
from under her.

THWUUUUMP!

The villain tripped and fell—right on top
of Gorilla Grodd!

Solomon Grundy slowed his charge as he
watched the pileup. Black Canary saw her
opening and took it.

EEEEEEEEEEEE!

The sonic scream shoved Grundy across
the floor. He slammed into his fallen
comrades.

The three villains rested in a heap of
tangled arms and legs.

But one foe was not finished fighting. Gorilla Grodd pushed aside the knocked-out Grundy and Giganta. The leader of the gang got back to his feet. A scowl twisted his primate face.

"I'll make you pay for all the trouble you've caused!" Gorilla Grodd shouted as he stomped toward Black Canary.

"Then I plan on ringing up a very big bill," Black Canary replied. "Because I'm not done making trouble yet!"

CHAPTER 5

LAST ONE STANDING

EEEEEEEEE!

Black Canary sent a sonic blast at
Gorilla Grodd. This time he braced against
the powerful sound. He stood like a pillar
of stone. Then he took a step forward.

EEEEEEEEEEEEEEE!

Black Canary increased the volume of
her Canary Cry. Grodd put his hands over
his ears and took another step toward her.

Still shouting her sonic song, the Super Hero leaped toward Gorilla Grodd and hit him with a flying kick. The blow, combined with the force of the Canary Cry, knocked the ape off-balance. He stumbled backward, spinning his arms to keep from falling.

Black Canary stopped her sonic blast, but just for a moment so she could grab one of Grodd's arms. She flipped him with an expert throw.

THWUUUUD!

The simian Super-Villain landed heavily on his back. He did not stay on the ground for long.

"I'm bigger and stronger than ten of you humans," Grodd boasted as he got to his feet once again. "You cannot defeat me!"

"Giganta was bigger than you, and I defeated her," Black Canary said. She tilted her head toward the unconscious villain. "You're not so tough."

"*Grrr!* I'll smash you like a bug!" Gorilla Grodd roared. He pounded his fists on the floor. The whole room shook.

"You know what? I have a better idea about what to smash," Black Canary replied.

EEEEEEEEEEEEEEE!

The hero sent a tremendous sonic blast at Gorilla Grodd. The surprised primate wasn't ready for it. The sound wave pushed him backward across the room and straight into the first computer bank. The machinery sparked and exploded.

BOOOOM! BLAAAM!

"*NOOO!* I just repaired that!" Gorilla
Grodd shouted.

Black Canary shrugged. "Oops."

Grodd snarled and launched himself
at Canary. She sidestepped his charge and
grabbed one of his ankles as he passed by.
A twist of her wrist sent him spinning
through the air.

The villain crashed into the second
computer bank. It exploded in a burst
of flames. *BOOM! BLAAAAM!*

Gorilla Grodd was furious. He picked
up a piece of the wreckage and threw it
at Black Canary. The hero backflipped out
of the way. The twisted metal hit the third
computer bank instead. *BOOM! BLAAAAM!*

Black Canary landed smoothly and smiled
at Grodd. "That's strike three. You're out."

Gorilla Grodd stood in shocked silence as he realized what had happened. He had been tricked into destroying his own computers!

"I can't believe you fell for all that. I thought you were supposed to be a super-genius," Canary said. "So much for world domination."

RAAAAAAR!

Gorilla Grodd became so enraged that he stopped thinking at all. He leaped at Black Canary like a wild animal.

The hero dodged the angry ape's attack and ran toward the door of the lab. She paused in the opening, looking down the hallway with the piston trap.

I wonder if any part of the trap is still working, Canary thought.

She stepped into the hall.

SMASSSH! BOOOOM! CRASSSH!

The few remaining pistons reactivated.
They shot in and out of the walls, floor,
and ceiling.

Good, it must have reset, Black Canary
thought as she started to move down the
hallway. *Grodd is so mad, I bet he'll run
straight into his own trap. I can use it to
take that big brute down!*

A moment later, Gorilla Grodd charged
over to the doorway. He roared with rage
when he saw the golden-haired hero running
away, jumping over the pounding pistons.

GRAAAAR!

Grodd chased after Canary. He smashed
at the walls and floor with his heavy fists
as he went. It did not matter what he hit.
He wanted to smash everything!

Black Canary reached the far end of the hallway. She stood with her back against the closed elevator doors and watched Gorilla Grodd barrel toward her. Even though only a few working pistons remained, Canary knew it would be enough.

Wall, ceiling, wall, floor, she repeated to herself.

EEEEEEEE! Canary timed her sonic blast just right. It threw the raging villain backward against a piston as it came out of the wall.

Gorilla Grodd slammed into the metal. He was dazed, but he was still extremely angry. He surged forward.

EEEEEEEEEEEEEE! Another Canary Cry tossed Grodd against a piston just as it flew down from the ceiling.

This time, Gorilla Grodd staggered. He dropped to the ground but quickly got back to his feet. He let out a growl and then kept lumbering forward.

Black Canary waited for a piston to come out of the wall again. Nothing happened.

Uh-oh. No more of those, she thought. *Okay. So floor is next.*

Just as Gorilla Grodd leaped toward the hero, the last working piston shot up from the floor.

EEEEEEEEEEEEEE! A third Canary Cry pushed Grodd into the piston.

THWUUUUMP!

Gorilla Grodd hit the piston with such force that the impact crushed the metal—and finally knocked out the furious foe. He fell to the floor.

The hallway became silent. The piston trap was completely destroyed. Black Canary walked through the wreckage to stand over the unconscious ape.

"Now look who's sleeping in your Super-Villain lair," Canary said.

She pulled a small communications device out from her jacket.

"I defeated you and your gang, stopped your evil plan, and saved the world. The only thing left to do is call the police," Black Canary told the knocked-out villain. "It's time to put you three baddies behind monkey bars."

THE ORIGINAL STORY:
GOLDILOCKS AND THE THREE BEARS

Once upon a time, there was a family of three bears. Papa Bear, Mama Bear, and Baby Bear lived in a house in the woods. One morning, they made some porridge. They went out for a walk to give it time to cool.

While they were gone, a girl named Goldilocks came by. When she saw no one was home, she walked right inside. The girl found the porridge on the table. She tasted each bowl. One was too hot. Another was too cold. But the third bowl was just right, and she ate it all up.

Then Goldilocks saw three chairs and decided to sit down. Papa Bear's chair was too hard. Mama Bear's chair was too soft. But Baby Bear's chair was just right. Soon, Goldilocks felt tired and went to the bedroom. The biggest bed was too hard. The medium-sized bed was too soft. But the smallest bed was just right. The girl fell asleep.

Later, the bears came home. Papa Bear saw that someone had tasted his porridge. Mama Bear saw that her bowl had been nibbled on too. But someone had eaten up all of Baby Bear's! The bears also noticed someone had been sitting in their chairs. Then they saw someone had been in Papa Bear's and Mama Bear's beds. Baby Bear saw that someone had been sleeping in his bed—and she was still there!

Goldilocks suddenly woke up to find the three bears staring at her. The girl jumped out of bed and ran out of the house. She never came back.

SUPERPOWERED TWISTS

- In the fairy tale, the three bears are kind and innocent. In this story, they are Super-Villains! Gorilla Grodd is Papa Bear, Giganta is Mama Bear, and simpleminded Solomon Grundy is Baby Bear.

- The family of bears leave their home to let their hot porridge cool down. The Super-Villains leave their hideout to steal more electronic equipment.

- Goldilocks goes into the bears' home to snoop around for no good reason. Black Canary sneaks into the villains' lair to investigate their evil scheme.

- The fairy tale girl tries out three bowls of porridge, three chairs, and three beds until she finds the one that's just right for her. Black Canary battles through three traps and tries to wreck three machines that are easy, harder, and finally too hard to destroy.

- Both golden-haired heroines run away at the end. But Black Canary runs away in order to lure Gorilla Grodd into his own trap so she can finally defeat him.

TALK ABOUT IT

1. If you could use only three words to describe Black Canary, which would you pick? Why? Support your answer with moments from the story.

2. Black Canary decides to investigate the villains' hideout alone. Do you think this was a good choice? What would you have done?

3. At the end, Gorilla Grodd becomes so angry that he stops thinking clearly and doesn't realize the danger of his own trap. In your own words, summarize why he was so furious.

WRITE ABOUT IT

1. Did the three villains make a good team? Write a paragraph explaining why or why not. Use examples to back up your answer.

2. Imagine you are a reporter. Write an article describing Grodd, Giganta, and Grundy's crimes and how Black Canary saved the day.

3. Fairy tales are often told and retold over many generations, and the details can change depending on who tells them. Write your version of "Goldilocks and the Three Bears." Change a lot or a little, but make it your own!

The Author

Laurie S. Sutton has been reading comics since she was a kid. She grew up to become an editor for Marvel, DC Comics, Starblaze, and Tekno Comics. She has written Adam Strange for DC, Star Trek: Voyager for Marvel, plus Star Trek: Deep Space Nine and Witch Hunter for Malibu Comics. There are long boxes of comics in her closet where there should be clothing and shoes. Laurie has lived all over the world and currently resides in Florida.

The Illustrators

Agnes Garbowska is an artist who has worked with many major book publishers, illustrating such brands as DC Super Hero Girls, Teen Titans Go!, My Little Pony, and Care Bears. She was born in Poland and came to Canada at a young age. Being an only child, she escaped into a world of books, cartoons, and comics. She currently lives in the United States and enjoys sharing her office with her two little dogs.

Sil Brys is a colorist and graphic designer. She has worked on many comics and children's books, having had fun coloring stories for Teen Titans Go!, Scooby-Doo, Tom & Jerry, Looney Tunes, DC Super Hero Girls, Care Bears, and more. She lives in a small village in Argentina, where her home is also her office. She loves to create there, surrounded by forests, mountains, and a lot of books.

GLOSSARY

acrobatic (ak-ruh-BAH-tik)—having to do with flips, rolls, handstands, and other gymnastic movements that require coordination and balance

brace (BREYS)—to get ready for something that is difficult; also, to press or push firmly against something

brute (BROOT)—a mean, beastlike person

enrage (en-REYJ)—to be filled with extreme anger

equipment (ih-KWIP-muhnt)—the machines and tools needed for an activity

frequency (FREE-kwuhn-see)—the number of wavelengths that pass by a fixed point each second; high frequency sounds have a high pitch and low frequency sounds have a low pitch

piston (PIS-tuhn)—a solid tubelike piece that slides in and out of a larger tube

simian (SIH-mee-uhn)—having to do with monkeys or apes

sonic (SON-ik)—having to do with sound

vibrate (VY-breyt)—to move back and forth quickly

wreckage (REH-kij)—the broken parts of something that has been damaged

READ THEM ALL!

DC SUPER HERO FAIRY TALES — THE AMAZON PRINCESS AND THE PEA
Sutton · Garbowska · Brys

DC SUPER HERO FAIRY TALES — SUPERGIRL AND THE CINDER GAMES
Sutton · Garbowska · Brys

DC SUPER HERO FAIRY TALES — BLACK CANARY AND THE THREE BAD BEARS
Sutton · Garbowska · Brys

DC SUPER HERO FAIRY TALES — LITTLE ROBIN'S FIGHTING HOOD
Stephens · Garbowska · Brys

DC SUPER HERO FAIRY TALES — BATMAN AND THE BEANSTALK
Stephens · Garbowska · Brys

DC SUPER HERO FAIRY TALES — BATMAN'S HANSEL AND GRETEL TEST
Stephens · Garbowska · Brys

DC SUPER HERO FAIRY TALES — AQUAMAN AND THE RAPUNZEL PLOT
Sutton · Garbowska · Brys

DC SUPER HERO FAIRY TALES — SUPERMAN AND THE RUMPELSTILTSKIN RUSE
Stephens · Garbowska · Brys